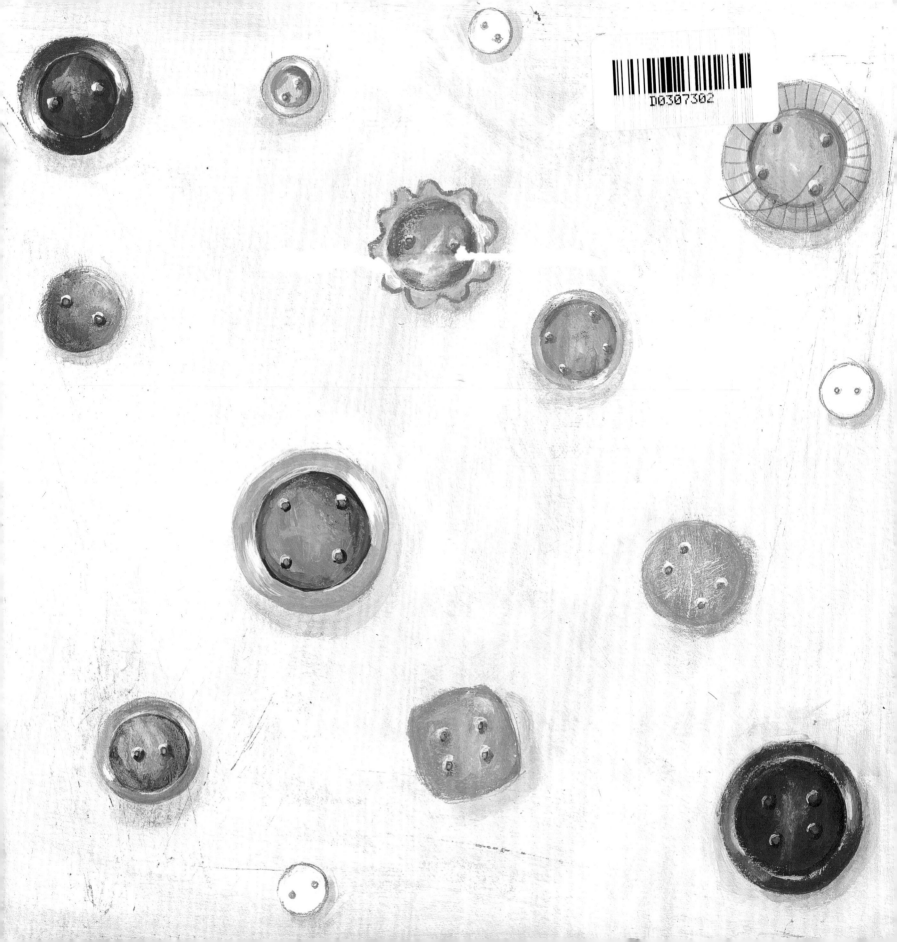

This book belongs to:

_____

_____

_____

For Will
L.M.G

For my family
R.S.

Thumbelina, first published 2008
The Snow Queen, first published 2008
The Elves and the Shoemaker, first published 2009

This edition first published 2010
by Meadowside Children's Books,185 Fleet Street, London, EC4A 2HS
www.meadowsidebooks.com

A CIP catalogue record for this book is
available from the British Library

10 9 8 7 6 5 4 3 2 1

Printed in China

# CLASSIC FAIRY TALE COLLECTION

Retold by Lucy M George and illustrated by Rachel Swirles

**meadowside**🍃
CHILDREN'S BOOKS

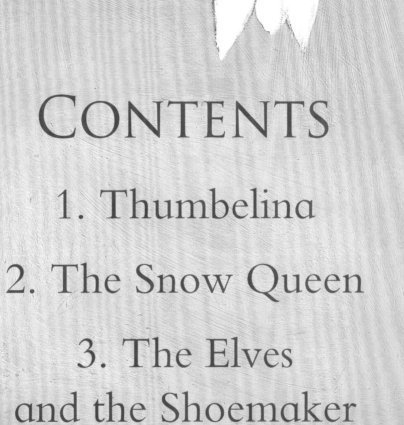

# CONTENTS

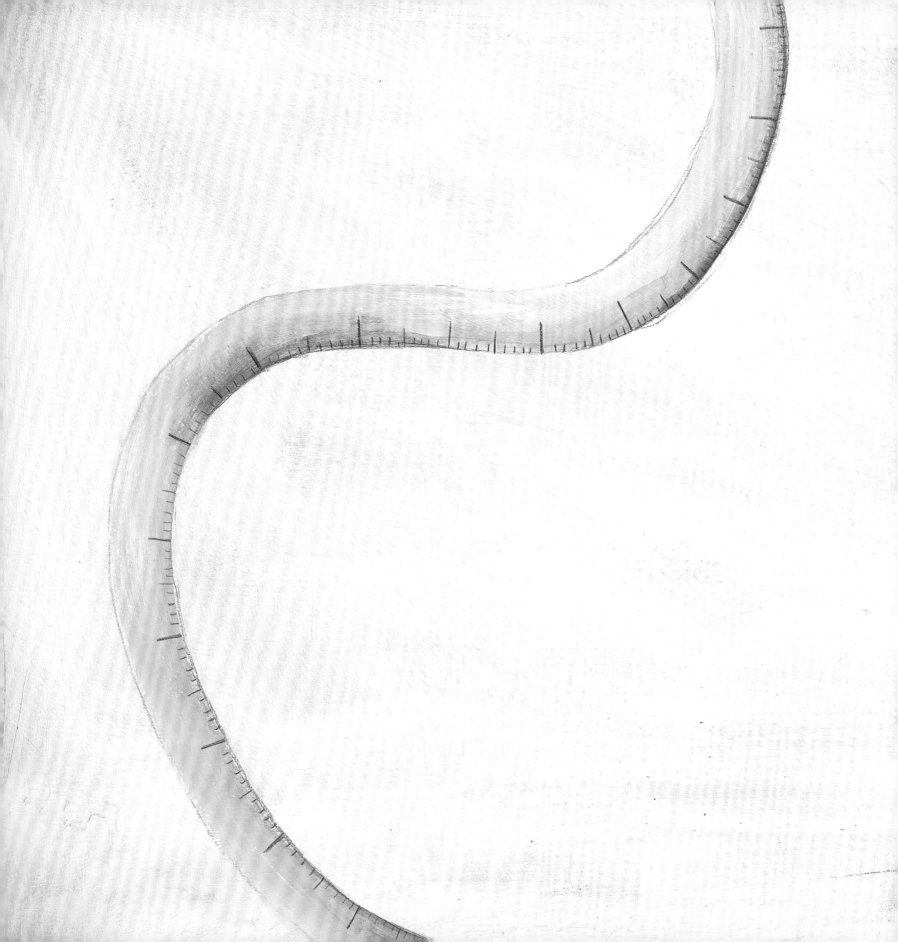

# THUMBELINA

Retold by Lucy M George and illustrated by Rachel Swirles

here was once a tiny little girl
who was no bigger than a thumb.
She was called Thumbelina.

She lived in a beautiful flower in a
warm and happy house.

On bright mornings she would
row across the milk bowl,
with a whistle and a giggle as she went,
smiling and happy with the world.

But one day,
as she slept beside
the window…

...a nasty toad mother
crept up and snatched her!

She trapped Thumbelina on a
lily leaf, too small to swim home,
too afraid to call for help.

The toad mother was going
to make Thumbelina marry
her horrid toad son!

As Thumbelina's tears splashed
into the pool, the fish looked up
and saw how lovely she was.
They had to help.

So they nibbled and they gnawed through the stem of the lily, until the leaf floated free.

"Oh thank you, thank you!" she called as she floated away.

But as she drifted, she realised that she was going further and further away from her home.

uddenly, a mayfly landed
on her leaf. Without even
saying 'hello', it poked her
and said, "My, my! You are
a pretty little thing, I think I shall
take you back to my family."

"Oooh!
It has no wings,"
said the mother.

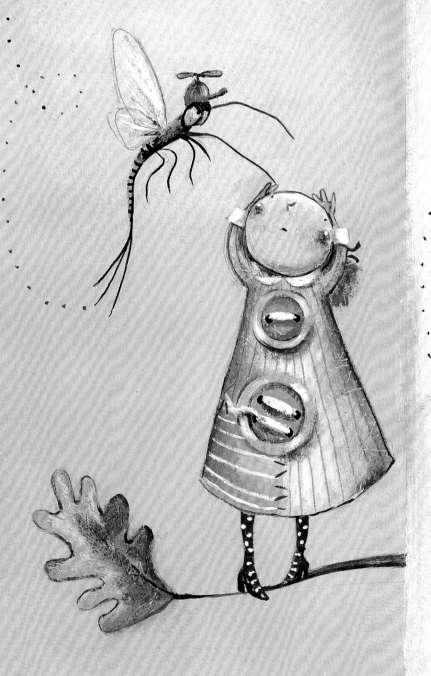

"Ergh!
It has no feelers,"
said the brother.

"Yuk!
It only has two feet,"
said the sister,
"and it is so ugly!"

They cast Thumbelina
from their tree.

**W**inter had come and
Thumbelina was all
alone in the world.

Great snow flakes fell
and the ground grew colder.

Shivering and hungry,
Thumbelina lay on
the frozen ground and wept.

Just as she was falling
into a deep, deep sleep…

…she felt a warm breath
upon her face.

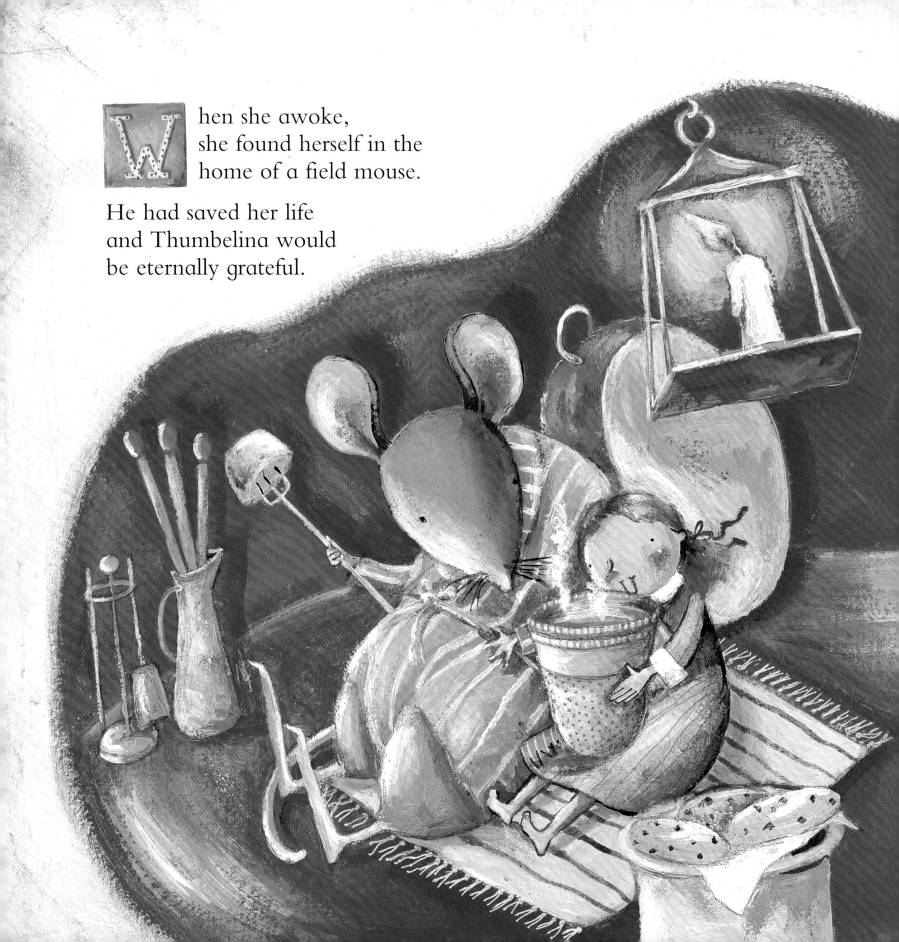

**W**hen she awoke,
she found herself in the
home of a field mouse.

He had saved her life
and Thumbelina would
be eternally grateful.

She and Mouse spent the whole winter
together, happy in his cosy little home.
Beside the merry little fire they were safe and
warm from the frosty winds outside.

that winter, Thumbelina would walk with Mouse to visit his friend Mole every afternoon for a cup of tea and homemade cakes.

They had a splendid time and Mole began to grow rather fond of Thumbelina.

Mole

Mouse was so kind to Thumbelina, but she soon found that he wanted her to repay him. The following year, Thumbelina would have to go and live with Mole in his dark underground hole!

ne day on the way to Mole's, Thumbelina heard a crying from the frosty earth above.

She crept to the surface and there, she found a small bird, lying in a tangled nest of twigs and leaves.

"I was too tired to fly with my friends this winter," cried the poor swallow.

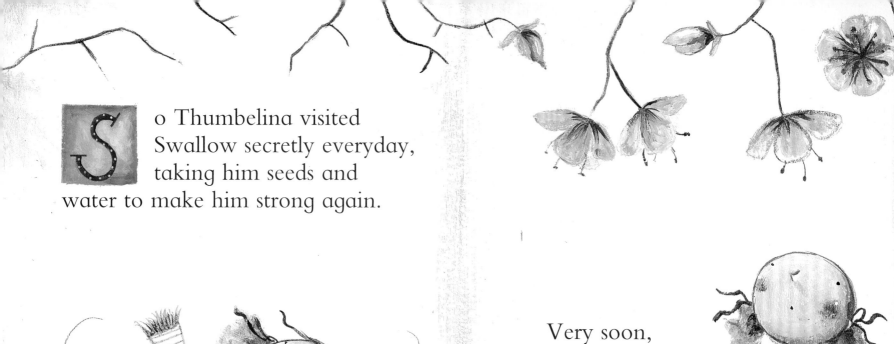

So Thumbelina visited Swallow secretly everyday, taking him seeds and water to make him strong again.

Very soon, they became the best of friends.

And over the seasons
that followed he slowly
got better and better.

Until, eventually,
Swallow was strong enough
to fly away.

"I will never forget you!"
he cried.
"And I will never
forget you!"
she said.

And she didn't.

But she missed him. And since
he had gone, Thumbelina had spent
all of her days inside with Mouse.
And now, the time had come to go
and live with Mole in his
dark underground hole.

Thumbelina
longed to see the sky
one more time, so she crept out
early one morning
whilst the ground was still soft.

A tear rolled down her cheek.
"Goodbye flowers!" she said sadly.

Suddenly, a bird landed beside her.
"Why are you crying?" he asked.
"Because," she wept, not looking up,
"I have to marry an old, blind mole tomorrow
and I'll have to live underground forever…"

He smiled and then, laughing gently, he said…

"Thumbelina! It's me!
Your old friend, Swallow!
You once saved me
and now I can save you."

Thumbelina threw her arms
around his neck and held on tightly.
Then they took off and soared away
from all her troubles.
Over mountains, past babbling brooks
and through fields,
dotted all over with wild
and colourful flowers.

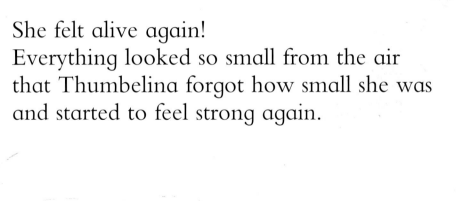

She felt alive again!
Everything looked so small from the air
that Thumbelina forgot how small she was
and started to feel strong again.

Then Swallow called out to her,
"Pick a flower!
That is where you shall live."

As they swooped towards the ground,
Thumbelina saw a beautiful
white flower.

"That one!" she pointed.

But as she fell softly into the flower,
Thumbelina gave a little cry of surprise.
For right there, in the middle was...

# The Prince
# of the Fairies!

Swallow waved goodbye
with a promise to visit her
every spring.

And so, at last,
Thumbelina had found
her home.

# THE
# SNOW QUEEN

Retold by Lucy M George and illustrated by Rachel Swirles

n a little town, not so far from here,
lived a boy and a girl. They were best
friends and their names were Kay and Gerda.

Kay and Gerda lived next door to one another.
From their windows they would play games,
pass secret notes, and talk all day,
(and sometimes whisper all night).

Everywhere they went, they went together. Everything they did, they did together. And every secret they had, they told each other. Every single one.

Kay loved the spring and Gerda loved the autumn,

but both of them loved the winter.

At the first sight of snow, they would drag Kay's
wonky old sledge to the hill and then ride it
all the way to the frozen lake, falling off
into the soft snow and laughing
as they went.

When it was cold enough
the lake froze so thick
that the children could
skate upon it.

ne day, some of the older children started talking about an evil queen. A queen who lived in the frozen hills. A queen who lived in a palace of ice.

The Snow Queen.

"She comes down here to steal children," said the oldest boy. "She blows enchanted snow into your face, then you have to go with her," he said.

"My grandmother told me she steals you from your bed and you can never come back because she makes you so cold, you forget who you are and where you live," said another one.

Kay was scared of the stories about the
Snow Queen and he told Gerda
on the way home.

"Nothing could ever make me forget you!"
promised Gerda. "Even if your heart
was frozen, and no one remembered you,
and you didn't even know who you were!
Even then.

I would remember you. I promise!"

And so they carried on up the hill, throwing snow, laughing and dreaming of the hot chocolate that awaited them at home, all thoughts of the Snow Queen gone.

One night, Gerda had a terrible nightmare. She was lost in the forest, shouting for Kay, but he was so far away, he seemed to be in another world. There was a reindeer trying to help her, but just as she was about to touch it, she awoke with a start.

She hurried into her winter
clothes and went outside
to meet Kay.

But he wasn't there.
No one was.

Instead, there was only a set
of wonky sledge tracks.
Kay's sledge tracks. And instead
of leading down to the lake,
they were leading up into the
frozen mountains.

Gerda rushed to Kay's
door but when his mother
answered it she didn't know
a boy called Kay.

No one knew
a boy called Kay.

Gerda pictured Kay alone
and afraid. She knew what
she had to do.

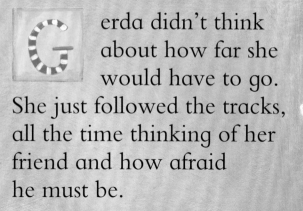Gerda didn't think about how far she would have to go. She just followed the tracks, all the time thinking of her friend and how afraid he must be.

She walked for many hours and snow began to fall, covering the tracks that Kay's sledge had left.

The harder she tried to picture Kay's laughing face, the harder the snow fell and the harder it became to follow his tracks, until eventually, the snow completely covered them.

She stood in the midst of a thicket of bracken and nettles and could only guess which way to go now.

ust as she felt all hope drain from her, something light seemed to move in the darkness.

A reindeer! It was warm and seemed so kind and gentle. Gerda was sure it was the reindeer from her dream. It was trying to help her.

She climbed onto its back
and it leapt forwards, carrying her
easily over the uneven frozen ground.
They pushed further and further into the frozen
mountains and just when Gerda thought that they
couldn't get any higher, they turned a corner.

An enormous palace of ice came into view.

Gerda could only gasp. It was the Snow Queen's
palace. It was true. She took a deep breath
and thought of Kay.

How afraid he must be!

Then she set off alone
across the frozen wasteland,
turning only to wave fondly
at the reindeer.

**S**ooner than she wished, Gerda was walking through the cold corridors of the Snow Queen's palace, silently padding over the frozen floor, desperately seeking Kay.

Strange noises echoed around the empty halls.

Then, she saw something.

It was Kay.
He was sitting on the cold floor,
staring into thin air.

"Kay, it's me!" she cried.

But Kay
just stared at her,
confused.

"Kay!" Gerda cried, shaking him, but he just looked at her blankly.

Gerda was helpless. She pulled at him, as if to try and drag him, but he was like a dead weight.

Finally, she fell to the floor, put her arms around her friend and sobbed.

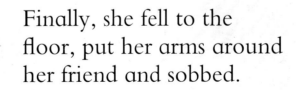

But as she cried,
her warm tears fell
onto Kay

and something
happened.

Kay's frozen heart began to melt, and the Snow Queen's evil spell was lifted.

Finally he knew who she was.

Kay smiled and laughed at the sight of his friend.
"You remembered me!"

**S**uddenly the Snow Queen appeared, screaming and trying to grab Kay back from Gerda.

"No!" she screeched wildly. "You cannot take him! He's mine!"

She was furious, but when she tried
to grab Kay, he was so warm that her
cold hands burned as she touched him!

There was no time to waste!

They sped through
the palace halls...

... and burst out into the fresh air.
The palace of ice had disappeared
and with it, the Snow Queen too.

She had been defeated!
Never again would she
be able to steal children.

And no one ever forgot what
Gerda had done for her friend,
especially not Kay!

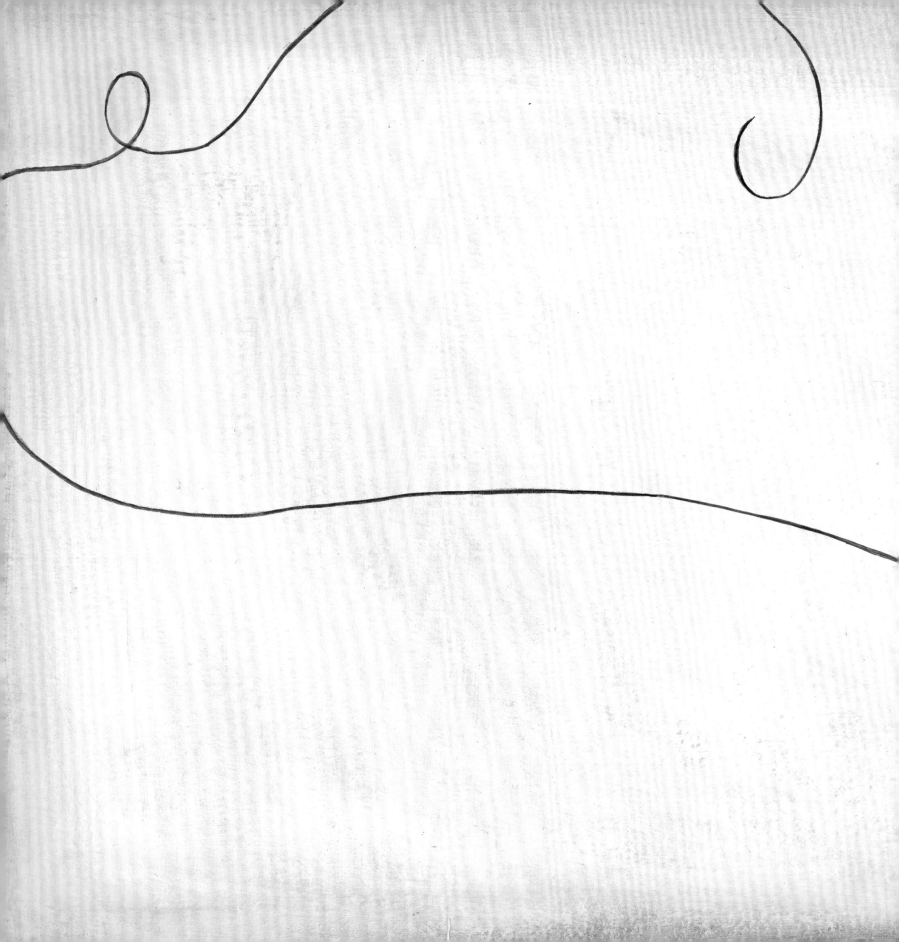

# THE ELVES AND THE SHOEMAKER

Retold by Lucy M George and illustrated by Rachel Swirles

There once lived a talented shoemaker. He lived with his wife in a little house, above a little shop, in a little town, above the rolling hills.

From far and wide, people came
to buy their beautiful shoes.

**T**he Shoemaker would spend all day drawing, cutting and stitching, filling the shop with wonderful shoes.

His wife would spend all day helping, searching and choosing, finding the perfect pair of shoes for each customer.

Each person would leave with a pair
of shoes that fitted and suited them
so perfectly, it was as if the shoes
had been made just for them.

he years passed happily,
and as they passed,
the Shoemaker grew older.

But as he grew older, his fingers did too.
He could no longer work as quickly
as he had once been able to.

Soon, a day came when they
sold their last pair of shoes.

The Shoemaker could only afford
enough leather to make one last pair.

As the sun was setting,
he carefully laid out
the last of his material.

He cut out the pattern,
paying attention to
every last detail.

Then he left the work
on his table and blew
out his candle.

Together the Shoemaker
and his wife climbed
to bed with heavy limbs
but faithful hearts.

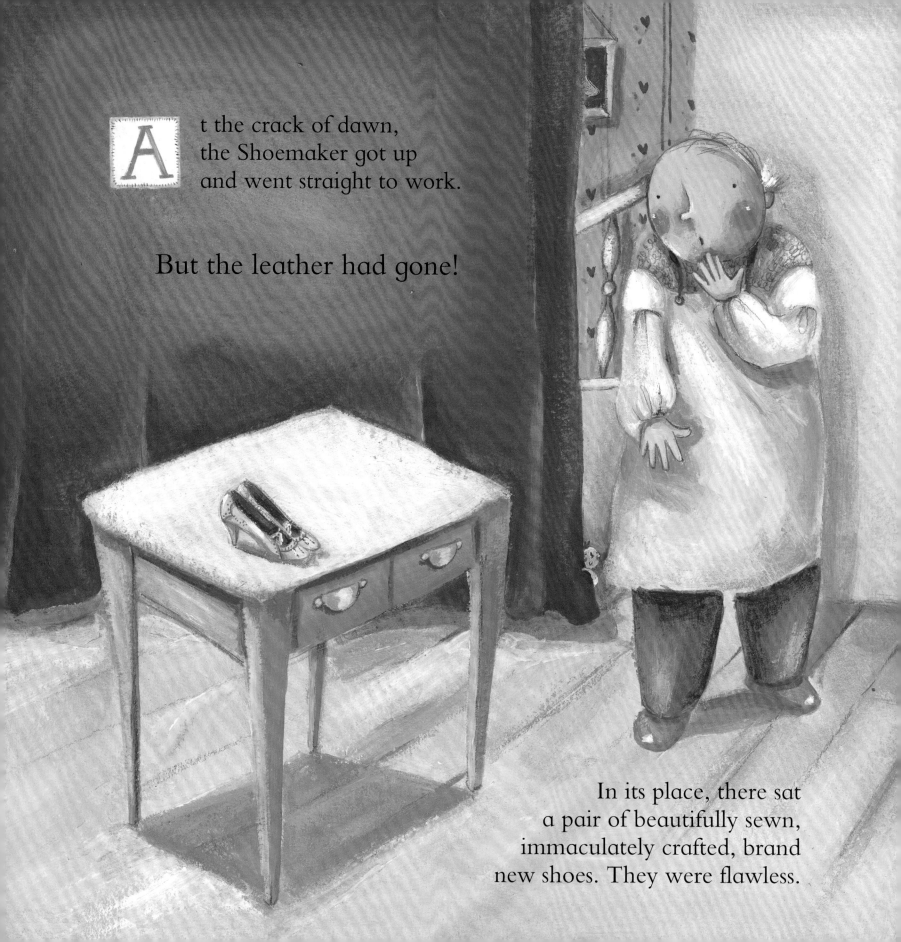

A t the crack of dawn, the Shoemaker got up and went straight to work.

But the leather had gone!

In its place, there sat a pair of beautifully sewn, immaculately crafted, brand new shoes. They were flawless.

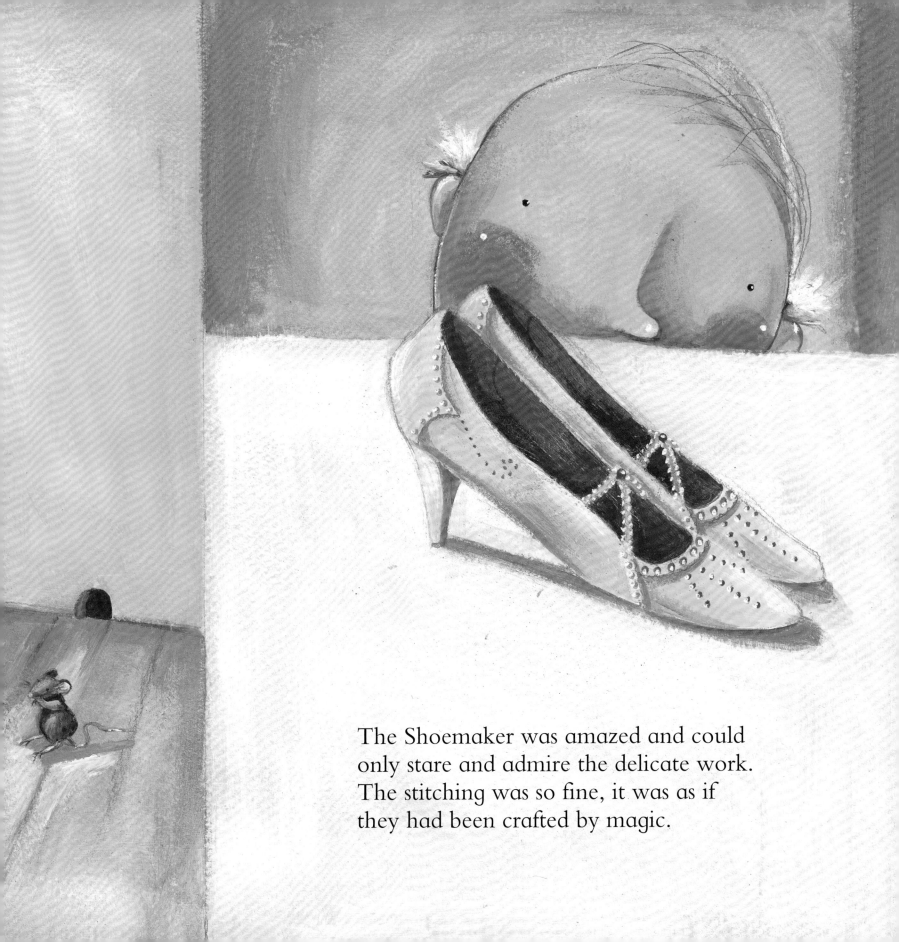

The Shoemaker was amazed and could
only stare and admire the delicate work.
The stitching was so fine, it was as if
they had been crafted by magic.

That day the Shoemaker's wife sold the shoes for twice the price she would normally get. The couple were overjoyed.

Shoemaker

The Shoemaker went straight out
and bought twice as much leather as the
day before. He cut it out and they went
to bed feeling encouraged
and inspired.

**T**he next morning, the Shoemaker went down to his workshop with a spring in his step.

But when he got there, he was amazed to see not one, but two extraordinary pairs of brand new shoes!

Before lunch time, both pairs had been sold for more than they had ever imagined possible.

The Shoemaker went out
and bought enough leather
to fill the shop with shoes
once more.

And for the rest of the
day he carefully cut out
the leather.

That night, the Shoemaker
and his wife decided to hide
and watch. They would wait
and discover who it was that
was helping them so kindly.
They crept behind a curtain
and silently waited.

As the clock struck twelve,
they heard the sound of
distant voices singing,
first softly, but getting closer.

Then in the dim light they saw…

…a group of tiny little elves!

They were dressed in
ragged clothes, their tiny feet
completely bare.

With perfect grace and the lightest touch,
the elves seized the leather, the needles
and the thread and stitched and sewed
and worked their nimble little fingers
so quickly it was enchanting.

When all the work was done,
the elves clapped their hands
and sang and danced in a merry circle,
skipping around the shoes with glee.

Such cheerful creatures had never been seen.

Such joyful singing
had never been heard.

Such handsome shoes
had never been made!

There were now enough shoes
to fill the shop again.

he Shoemaker and his wife knew they had to do something to show how grateful they were. Then they had an idea.

They worked all day long, drawing, cutting and sewing...

...until finally,
when the sun had set,
their work was complete.

Late that night
they went back to
their old hiding place
and quietly waited.

As the clock struck twelve,
they saw the elves,
in their ragged old clothes,
dance into the shop.

But when they reached the table,
their singing suddenly stopped
as it was replaced with excited
chatter and squeals of joy.

On the table lay a tiny
little outfit for each of them,

and a pair of shoes
each too!

When they were dressed,
the elves began to sing.
They danced, admired each
other, and giggled and squealed!

How fine they all looked!

The couple watched with smiles
of pride as the elves, still giggling
and dancing, took off into the night.

**T**he shop was flourishing again, filled with beautiful shoes and excited customers...

...and the Shoemaker and his wife lived happily once more!

But from then on,
once in a while, when the
Shoemaker had a little spare
leather and a little spare
time, he would make a pair
of tiny shoes and leave them
out for the elves…

…and sure enough, once in a while, there would be a little surprise on the Shoemaker's table in the morning!

THE END